T0132360

A BOY NAMED JAKE

Trene Plowman

Balboa Press books may be ordered through booksellers or by contacting:

Balboa Press
A Division of Hay House
1663 Liberty Drive
Bloomington, IN 47403
www.balboapress.com
844-682-1282

ISBN: 978-1-9822-6643-1 (sc)
ISBN: 978-1-9822-6644-8 (e)

Library of Congress Control Number: 2021906635

Print information available on the last page.

Balboa Press rev. date: 04/14/2021

Contents

Dedication

This book and these stories are dedicated to my parents; Bonnie and Gerald Plowman and to my grandparents; Clarence, Enid Alice, John and Cora, my incredible siblings and their families, and my own beautiful family... All of you are my true treasures.

I have deep gratitude for the gift of life, our precious family, the beautiful place we grew up, and the wisdom, stories, love and laughter so freely taught and shared.

I love and honour you all.

The Best Helper

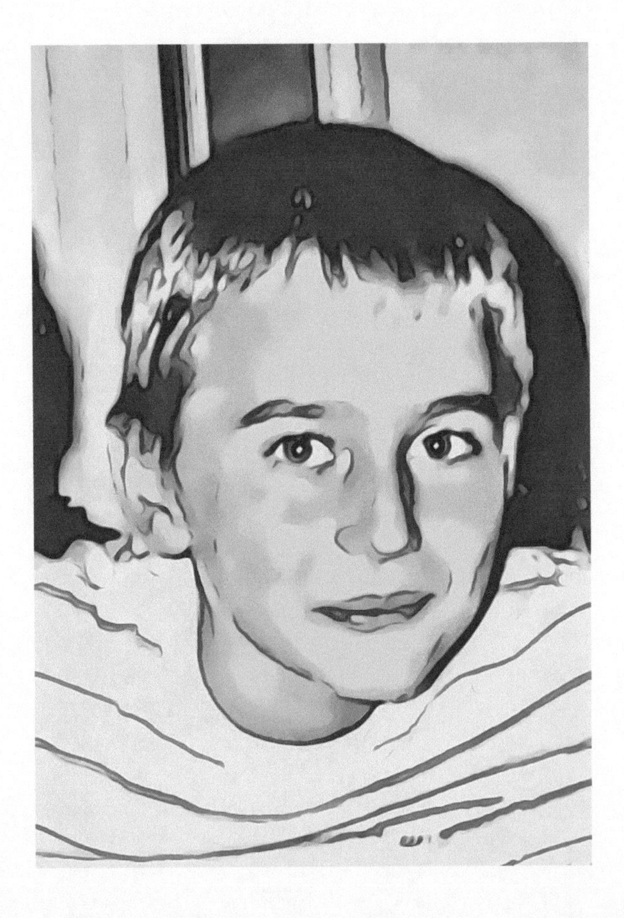

"This bag sure is heavy", the little boy thought. Jake was strong for five years old and was used to helping out around the house, but this was really HARD! The hill was about a quarter of a mile long and he was getting close to the top of the dusty incline, his little face determined and smudged with dirt and sweat. He brushed his blonde hair out of his eyes with the back of a grubby hand and looked up at the sun. "Boy....it's hot!"

He crested the hill and saw home. His Mom probably had lunch ready; she always had lunch ready when the sun was straight overhead. Jake shifted the load in the bag and began the gentle descent to the house sitting near the trees. "It sure is easier going downhill" Jake thought, and walked just a little faster...his Mom's lunches were always delicious, and he had worked up an appetite!

He pulled at his jeans, hiking them up to his waist with one hand; his Mom said he was too skinny and that was why his pants were always slipping. Jake was sure she would be upset about the big hole in the behind of his brand new jeans, but she always forgave him when he explained how slippery it was by the creek, or some other perfectly reasonable accident.

Jake was smiling now, excited about the treasure that he dragged behind him! (and wow, was it heavy!) Jake and his Mom had been working on this new project for a week or so now, and this would finish it just right! "Mom isn't going to believe I did this all by myself" he thought.

He left the bag near their worksite and ran to the house; his shoelaces flapping as he ran. The door banged open as he ran through. "Mom!" he called, "I got them, I got them!" His Mom came around the corner from the kitchen. "What is it Jake? Are you ok?' Jake"s face was beaming with excitement and happiness. "Come quick, you"ve got to see!!"

Jake and his Mom went outside and he pulled her by the hand all the way to the worksite. He opened the burlap bag and began removing the flat creek rocks one by one; ten in all. "Look Mom, the rest of the rock for our vegetable garden!" he said with a huge, brilliant smile. "I got them all so we can finish our project!"

"Oh Jake," his Mom hugged him tight, "I could never ask for a better helper."

The Dog

Jake had always wanted a dog. A dog to play with, and roam the countryside around their house with. Jake was an only child; a spunky blonde five year old with bright sparkling blue eyes and a broad cheerful face, tanned from hours outside in the sun. He just knew that a dog would be the perfect companion for all his adventures, but his Mom was hard to convince.

Jakes's Mom was great! She and Jake were a team; busy in the house and the yard with projects, and he always helped if she wanted him to. The thing was, some stuff was more just for boys. Like tree climbing and hunting for aliens and catching grasshoppers and ladybugs and hiding from the Sasquatch that old Mr. Newton said lived in the trees past the creek. That was where the dog would come in. A sidekick, a posse, and even a pack animal for his six-shooters and water bottles. And a dog would be a darn good lookout if that sassy Sasquatch came to get him!

Molly, (that was Jake's Mom) said that Jake was becoming very responsible but she wasn't sure he could handle a dog. He left his shoes in the creek, he forgot his dress-up sweater outside in the garden and his Mom said he never remembered to brush his teeth; so she was certain he couldn't remember to feed and water a dog. Jake had been trying very hard to show his Mom that he would take good care of a dog, and he had even asked his Uncle Mark about helping him to train the dog when he got one. Uncle Mark had two dogs, and he had trained them both...all by himself!!! His Uncle said he would be happy to help him, as long as Molly said it was ok.

Jake squinted into the distance. He could see the slow drift of smoke from the chimney of their house, and he hiked up his jeans and started for home. Every other step he took, he tossed a rock into the bushes. The pockets of his jeans were full of pebbles that he collected every time he went to the creek; and this, combined with the fact that he was skinny (that's what his Mom said) had him hiking his pants up constantly. He collected the pebbles and threw them as he walked to scare off animals that might be lurking! (and of course... Sasquatches!!!)

He was just approaching the yard when a long cloud of dust and loud rock music signalled the arrival of Uncle Mark. Jake love the old blue Chevy, and he really loved when his Uncle let him sit on his lap and drive all the backroads with the music blaring and the dogs barking! He hoped he could have that truck when he got a license... he didn't even care that the tailgate was held on with a rope!

Uncle Mark jumped down from the truck and swung Jake high over his head. "Hey Nascar 2, how's it going?" He ruffled Jakes's hair with his hand as they turned to see Molly coming out of the house. Jake responded, "pretty good Nascar 1, how come you're here? Are you staying for supper?

His Uncle laughed his big booming laugh. "slow down boy, I can't get a word in edgewise!" Molly laughed. "You sure are staying for supper after coming out here on such important business!" She winked at Jake. "We can't let a special delivery man leave hungry, now can we Jake?" "No Ma'am," Jake replied "but what did you special deliver Uncle Mark?" as he turned to his uncle and cocked his head to the side, one hand hiking up his jeans.

"Well, I was down in the city last weekend and I found me a new friend, so I thought I'd bring her out to meet you Nascar 2." Mark turned back to the old Chevy and Jake noticed a cage he hadn't seen before strapped into the back of the truck. His uncle hopped up into the bed of the truck and undid the latch on the cage. "This is Sniffer' he said. "Sniffer...meet Jake."

A beautiful Golden Retriever stepped gracefully from the cage and walked straight over until she was nose to nose with Jake. She sat down and nudged Jake's ear with her nose. "I think she likes you Jake" said Molly. "Can I pet her Mom?" he asked. "Of course honey, she loves children, and she sure seems gentle with you".

Jake reached out his hand and softly stroked her silken head. The gentle creature sniffed him all over. "That's why they called her Sniffer" laughed his Uncle. "Why don't the two of you go play and I'll help your Mom with supper" he suggested. Jake looked at his Mom and she nodded.

"Come on Sniffer!!" he called, and the two of them dashed up the slope away from the yard. "Man, is he going to burst when he realizes the dog is his!" Mark and Molly laughed, and watched as the blonde boy and his dog played and wrestled in the grass.

"Don't be too long Jake, supper is almost ready!" his Mom called. Jake and Sniffer both turned to look at her; cocking their heads to the side. "OK Mom,' he yelled "we'll be back soon!", and they ran together over the hill.

The Garden

"That's it Jake" said his Mom "easy does it now," and together they lowered the last rock down into the spot they had prepared. The blond haired pair had been working all morning on their vegetable garden, placing the rocks in a rectangle that later they would fill with a truck load of soil. "We did it Mom!" Jake said proudly. Molly smiled and stood back to survey their work. "We sure did buddy, and it looks terrific!" she exclaimed. "Now let's go have some lunch, and by then Uncle Mark will be here with the soil" she suggested, and taking Jake's hand they headed for the house.

They were just finishing their grilled cheese sandwiches and tomato soup when a booming voice called out "Hey! Does anybody here need some dirt?" Jake jumped up from the table and ran toward the cheerful looking man coming through the door. "Uncle Mark! Did you see how good we did?" he asked as his Uncle gave him a bear hug. "I sure did Nascar 1, it looks SUPER!" his Uncle praised.

Mark, Molly and Jake went out to the garden, putting on work gloves and gathering shovels and hoes. Uncle Mark had backed his old pickup truck up to the rock wall of the garden and removed the tailgate which was held onto the blue Chevy with a length of rope. Jake climbed into the bed of the truck and pushed the dirt forward, Uncle Mark shoveled it into the rock enclosure, and Molly spread it evenly around in their new garden. Jake inhaled as he pushed the warm, moist soil to the back of the truck. He loved the smell of it and loved to work in it with his Mom and her brother and watch things grow. He had even collected 10 of these rocks all by himself for their garden project, and he was very proud of the work they had done. Jake could hardly wait to get planting.

It took an hour to unload the truck and another hour to finish spreading the dirt and mixing in the extras like the fertilizer Molly had purchased from the neighbours farm. The trio cleaned up the site, had showers and then a good dinner. Molly said they would plant all their seeds tomorrow. Jake was disappointed they didn't get to plant any seeds today...but it really had been a tiring day...so he guessed his Mom was right, and it was dark now.

Jake fell asleep with his head on his Mom's lap on the couch. They were watching a movie; but he was so sleepy he just couldn't keep his eyes open. His sleep that night was filled with dreams. Dreams of the earth and gardens, of water and sunshine. Seeds and planting. Vegetables that grew so big, they were taller than him... and double carrots of different colours! His vegetables were filled with goodness, and helped people stay healthy.

When Jake woke the next morning, he knew what he wanted to be when he grew up. A Master Gardener!

The Tree Swing

Jake and Sniffer went everywhere together. They were best friends and Jake always felt safe when the beautiful Golden Retriever was with him. Sniffer was a loyal and gentle friend, and she loved Jake, Molly and Uncle Mark with all of her brave heart.

Today, the pair had a picnic lunch packed by Jake's Mom, Molly and they were headed to the creek. There was a grassy clearing with one big shade tree along the rocky bank and that was their spot. Jake had a big length of rope with him today; his plan was to create a tree swing in the strong branches of the big shade tree. He figured if he did it just right, he may be able to swing to the other side of the creek and see if once and for all he could find signs of the Sasquatch that old Mr. Newton told him was living in the trees there.

Sniffer roamed on either side and ahead of Jake as she always did; never farther than ten feet away from her boy, but always making sure there was no danger. In the four years she had lived with him, Jake had gotten into quite a bit of mischief and it was up to her to protect him, so she never went very far from her blonde-haired charge. The two of them started to trot now, the creek was close and they were anxious to get there. Birds scattered left and right as the tow-headed pair burst into the clearing, Jake laughing at Sniffers bounding and leaping, and her readiness to wrestle on the cool grass. "you sure love to wrestle, don't you girl?" He smiled and gave Sniffer a hug.

The two wrestled for a time, and then Jake settled down to the business of the tree swing. He tied a knot about three feet from the end of the rope for a handle and a larger knot at the end for a foot rest. Then he looped the rope around and around his body like a sash and started his climb up into the branches. It was an easy climb for the 10 year old, he had done it so many times he was familiar with each and every hand-hold and foot rest on the grand old tree. Sniffer lay panting in the shade; surveying the clearing and beyond, protecting her boy.

The rope dropped down as Jake shouted "watch out Sniffer!" He shimmied down the rope, stopping with his foot on the knot. He started to swing. "This is great!" he thought. "Look Sniff...it works!!" His bright blue eyes twinkled with glee. "I did it!!!"

The rope was long enough that it swung Jake all the way to the opposite bank of the creek. "Come on Sniff!" Jake called, "lets go over", and he gave one mighty swing and jumped as he approached the grass. He landed easily on his feet, rolled once, and stood back up. He hiked up his jeans and looked back toward the creek. Sniffer was wading across the shallow spot just above the falls, where the 4 foot creek narrowed before the water poured over the rocks. "Wow! That was fun, I wish you could do that with me Sniff" he smiled. Jake ruffled the fur on the gentle girl's head, and she licked his face. 'Now, lets go see if we can find that Sasquatch!'

Jake and Sniffer headed into the trees. The sunlight streamed down through the branches; dappled and mysterious as it narrowed and filled with the bits of dust, pollen and other indistinguishable matter that floated in the air. The shadows...that was where Jake imagined the Sasquatch to be. Slipping silently from tree to tree, they made their way in a zig-zag pattern down the edge of the forest; but after a half an hour hunger won out over the search.

Jake swung back over the creek and Sniffer followed below. They enjoyed the lunch that Molly had prepared for them, and then Jake looked up at the sky. "Time to go Sniffer, I have to milk the goats and clean my room." He gathered up all of his belongings and trash, and then tied the end of his rope swing to the big tree.

"C'mon girl!" he called out and Sniffer reluctantly turned away from the creek's edge and followed Jake toward home. Sniffer stopped; nose in the air, sniffing the wind. Jake disappeared into the trees and Sniffer followed, stopping once more and looking back across the creek... her nose in the air.

"SNIFFER"!!!!!!!!!

She responded immediately to his call; that boy she loved more than anything, but she knew they had been close to something...or someone. Something unfamiliar. Something curious.

From the shadows of the thick trees across the water; hidden except for the slow blink, a pair of big round eyes watched them go.

Jake's New Friend

Jake brushed the damp hair out of his eyes with the back of his just-bathed hand. "Mom, these jeans won't stay up!" he hollered as he hiked up his pants after fastening the snap. "Jake, stop hollering please" his Mom scolded. "Your jeans never stay up because you are too skinny yet, but you will grow. If we buy them to fit your waist, they will only come to your knees. Now finish getting dressed so we can go and meet our new neighbours." Jake smiled. "Yes Ma'am" he said.

Molly tousled his hair. "You are going to make a new friend today buddy." Then she quickly ran upstairs to quickly finish getting ready too. Jake was happy to be meeting the neighbours. They had a little girl 10 years old just like him, and they would even go to school together this fall! Mr. Newton; the old man who always sat outside the Post Office and knew everyone and their stories, said she was a nice girl and as brown as a berry from the sun. Jake hoped that meant she liked to play outside...a LOT, and he hoped she wasn't fussy like that little Lila Mae Brady. She was a real pain...even for a girl.

"Jake, hurry now' his Mom said as she sailed into the kitchen to retrieve the cake she had made for the Nielsons. Molly said you should never go anywhere empty-handed, and always bring something yummy for people who are moving or working. Jake finished putting on his shoes. "I'm ready Mom" he said, and held the door for her as she came through with a gorgeous chocolate cake. "Mmmmmm" Jake said. It smelled delicious.

The Nielson's place was abuzz with people. Jake thought it was like a beehive. Mrs. Neilson was in the middle of the yard directing everyone, her black curly hair in a ponytail that didn't control it much. A tall and skinny, very pale man was in the barn...taking lessons from another man on how to milk a cow and a goat. Molly said that was Mr. Nielson, and that he and his wife had never lived on a farm before, so they might need some help. Jake's Mom parked the car out of the way of all the busyness, and they got out.

After the phone and utility trucks left, and the lesson for milking the animals had ended, everyone gathered in the bright green kitchen and Janice Nielson put on a pot of coffee. "I thank you so much for the lovely cake Molly,' she smiled."and I'm sure Paige is around here somewhere Jake" She walked to the bottom of the stairs. "Paige!!" she called, "you have company!"

A petite girl with dark curly hair and impish green eyes appeared at the top of the stairs as if by magic. "Coming Mama" she sang, and with a flourish, she slid down the bannister and landed squarely on both feet. "HI!" she said to Jake and extended her hand. "I'm Paige, and I'm pleased to make your aquaintance." Jake was delighted! Here was a girl with possibilities! "I'm Jake, and we brought cake!" and they shook hands and giggled at his accidental poem.

After cake and a glass of ice cold milk the new friends headed out for the barn. Molly, Janice and Terrence (you can call me Terry) stayed comfortably chatting in the kitchen over their coffees. The barn was full of goats in pens; with food and water and comfortable places to sleep, and one cow that Paige said her Mom and Dad wanted for milk and butter. The goats were for the Nielson's new business...goat's milk, cheese and soap that Paige's Mom would take to the city and sell to stores. Paige said they were going to be rich, just as soon as they learned to milk the animals.

The whole time they talked, they climbed. Up the ladder to the loft. then up another ladder into the rafters, where five boards were securely nailed from rafter to rafter creating another loft, just the perfect size for the two of them. "This is cool Paige" Jake said in an admiring fashion. Paige smiled. "this can be our lookout!" she said, and Jake agreed. "We can watch for goat thieves and robbers and stuff from up here" he said. "yeah" she nodded, we can even see the house if we are down in the loft,' and she headed down the ladder. The happy friends spent some time setting up their fort with extra boards and some blankets, (in case it gets cold) and got a set of walkie-talkies from Paige's room for their 'spy headquarters'.

Then Paige took Jake around to the backyard, and Jake was delighted to see a swing set and a trampoline! "WOW!!! I have always wanted a trampoline!" he exclaimed. Paige laughed. "well, now you can use this one anytime you want, AND my Dad says we can be on it alone because of the safety cage." The pair scrambled up and onto the bouncy surface and began to take turns jumping "I feel like I'm flying!" Jake yelled.

"This is great Jake! I am so glad you came over!" Paige sang. Jake had to agree. This had sure turned out to be a terrific day. He had an amazing new friend, and she wasn't fussy at all!

The Big Fish

Jake dumped one last scoop of the warm, moist soil over the worms he had collected in his silver pail. "This is going to be a great day!" he thought; a bright, wide smile lighting up his tanned face. He headed at a run to where his Uncle Mark was waiting with Jake's Mom, Molly. "yep, today is the day!" Jake was going to catch a fish...A BIG FISH!

"There you are Nascar 2, did you get em?" Uncle Mark asked. "yes Sir, I sure did...big, fat, wiggly ones that the fish will love!" Jake beamed. He put the bucket down and hiked up his pants. Jake was always hiking his pants up to where they belonged; his Mom said he was just skinny now but that he would grow and fill out the trousers soon. Jake was tall for 5 years old, with an active imagination and bright blue eyes that never missesd a thing. Uncle Mark fished a worm out of the bucket. "Look at this would you Molly. Jake got some juicy ones!" Mark laughed. "The fish won't be able to resist those Jake." Molly smiled as she hugged him to her.

Mark and Jake gathered their supplies and headed for the creek. Molly watched the two blonde heads disappear over the hill, and then covering her own blonde hair with a large hat and donning her work gloves she went into the garden to pull weeds. Molly also planned to get some vegetables to go with the fish she hoped the guys would bring home for dinner. "That will be a nice surprise for them" she smiled to herself as she knealt to her work.

Uncle Mark and Jake chatted all the way to the creek; discussing how big the fish might be, how hard they would fight, and how long they may have to wait for even a nibble. "Fishin' is a lot like life Jake," Uncle Mark told him. "Sometimes you have to be real patient about things, but it is worth it in the end.' Jake smiled. Uncle Mark was so smart...in fact, besides his Mom he was probably the smartest person Jake knew.

They arrived at the edge of the creek, just up from the clearing where the flow narrowed and boiled over the rocks. THE FALLS. "The Falls" were only a couple of feet high, but when the fast water slammed into the rocks and hit and churned in the water below it created a foam the would sometime stand 18 inches high! The foam looked like bubbles in a bathtub, but white and light brown in colour; with bits of leaves and sticks and dirt caught in its gauzy structure. It was shady here, and peaceful...and Jake loved it. His Uncle said it was the perfect place to catch a fish.

They cut two sturdy willow branches for poles, and tied fishing line to the ends. Uncle Mark showed Jake how to tie a hook to the end of the line, and how to be careful placing the worm on the hook. Jack tried it twice before he got it to stay. Those worms sure were slippery! Finally, they were ready. They dropped their lines into the water under the foam; in the eddy created by the flow of the water, and settled down to wait.

tug-tug...TUG!

Jake felt the two gentle nibbles and then the fish HIT! "hold him Jake!!" Uncle Mark grabbed for the fish net as Jake brought his pole around. "Keep the tip of your pole up." Jake did as instructed, and soon the shimmering, wriggling, tail flapping creature was securely in the net! "GOOD JOB Nascar!" his Uncle yelled excitedy. Jake felt his face grow warm and his hands were tingling. It felt like Christmas morning! Jake's face beamed with pride.

"I did it Uncle Mark! I did it!" Jake got another worm out of the pail and carefully baited his hook. "I'm going to catch enough for supper" he stated. His Uncle smiled. "Yes Nascar, I believe you will. I believe you will."

The Pocket Watch

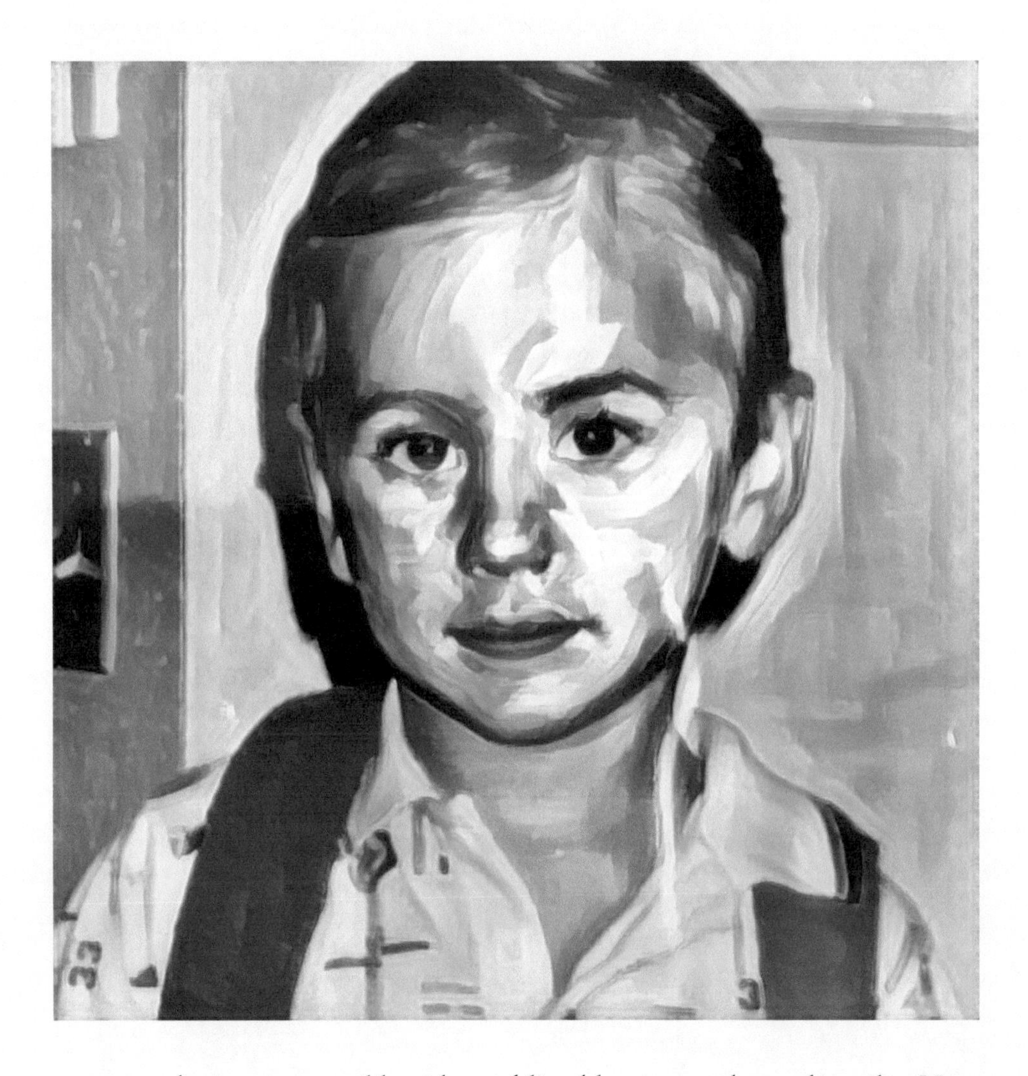

Jake was a strong and wiry six year old, with sparkling blue eyes and a ready smile. He was curious and energetic, spending most of his time busy...and usually accompanied by his Golden Retriever, Sniffer. Today though, he was quiet. Jake had been in his room all day, and there was no sparkle in his eyes; not even when Sniffer nuzzled her cold, wet nose into him or licked his hand.

Jake was sad, and he was sad because he had lied. He had stolen something from Mr. Newton and then he lied about it. Jake was very upset with himself. Mr. Newton had always been a very good friend to Jake; letting him come over and stay, teaching him to whittle, showing him how to fix the lawnmower and telling him Sasquatch stories. Jake was so sorry he had taken the pocket watch; it had just been an impulse, but once it was done he just didn't know how to undo it!

The little blonde haired boy reached into the pocket of his jeans and pulled out the beautiful watch. It was very old, with a golden stag in the trees carved into the gold on one side and a river with an eagle in flight on the other. Inside it said, "To Ralph, love Mom and Dad." A single tear ran down each of Jake's cheeks and met in one large drop on his chin, where it hung shaking from the quivering of his lip until it dropped onto the watch face.

KNOCK-KNOCK-KNOCK

"Jake?" his Mom said as she pushed open the door. "Are you OK Bud?" she asked when she saw her son sitting silently on the edge of the bed. "Are you crying honey?" and she crossed the room and sat besde Jake, putting her arm around his shoulders. Jake slowly pulled his hand out of the pocket he had quickly jammed it into when his Mom entered the room. He opened his hand, palm up; and revealed his terrible secret.

"Oh Jake,' his Mom had such sadness in her voice. "I cannot believe you took Ralph's watch from him," Molly sounded so disappointed, "and then you lied to us about it too!" Another pair of tears followed the first to Jake's chin, followed by more and more... and more. "I'm so sorry Mom, I just wanted one, and this is so nice and I didn't think anyone would really care!" he cried.

Molly stood up. "Allright young man,' she said quietly, "we are going over to Mr. Newton's house so you can return the watch to him." Jake stood up slowly. "Do I have to Mom?" he said in a very small and soft voice. "Yes son...you do" Molly answered gently. She put her arm around Jake's shoulders and they walked together to the car.

Ralph Newton saw the car approaching and put down the stick he was whittling. He walked down the wide porch steps and waited. Molly parked the car, she and Jake got out, and they walked toward him. Molly waited at the end of the path, and Jake and Mr. Newton met each other half way.

"Hello Jake," Ralph said. "I didn't expect you to be back so soon." and he smiled at the small boy. Once again Jake removed his hand from his picket and held it palm up. "I'm so sorry Mr. Newton" he said simply. The gold watch glinted in the afternoon sun. "Oh my," Mr. Newton shook his head slowly. "I am very surprised you took my watch Jake, but i am very glad you are returning it,' and he reached out and put his hand over the watch.

"I swear I'll never steal again Sir." Jake promised, and looked Ralph straight in the eyes. "See that you don't Jake," Mr. Newton said softly. "A man of honour does not take what is not his." He paused and then extended his right hand.

As the two friends shook hands, Mr. Newton smiled his crooked half-smile. "I am proud of you for standing up and admitting what you did." he said. Molly walked up to the duo and put her hand on her son's arm. "So am I Jake" she nodded.

Jake smiled. His eyes began to twinkle again.

The Surprise

Jake was SO excited! He and his Mom were going somewhere for a surprise, and Molly would not even give him a hint except that it would be a fabulous day! She was such a good secret-keeper...there was no way she would tell him anything...so Jake finished getting dressed and grabbed his yellow backpack.

"I'm ready Mom!" Jake called out. "Come in here please Jake, and get your lunch for your backpack" his Mom replied. A lunch of sandwiches, 2 of his Mom's famous cookies, an apple, and his favourite bottle filled with water went into his backpack with his mittens and touque. "Come on now honey" Molly said, we cannot be late!"

Two hours later they pulled into a parking lot at a TRAIN STATION! It was a beautiful old train... all made of wood; even the seats, driven by a real engineer, and the train was Jake's favourite colour; yellow! When they heard the Conductor's loud call of "ALL ABOAAARD!" Jake thought he would erupt with happiness! He pulled his jeans back up to his waist with one hand and climbed the stairs into their train car.

It was a prettier journey than Jake had even imagined! Over bare ground, through thick woods, and even along the edge of a cliff! His Mom, Molly, said they were perfectly safe, even though he kind of felt a bit dizzy when he looked down! They arrived at the top of the mountain after 1.5 hours, and the Conductor said they had 4 hours to explore, eat and shop before the train left for the ride back down the mountain.

The blonde-haired pair puttered about in the wee town for about an hour, and Jakes' Mom even bought him a special gift! A silver chain necklace, made from silver mined right there on the mountain! Then his Mom said she wanted to show him a special place, and they set out on a hike away from the town, into the woods.

It was almost silent as they left the bustling sounds of the town behind, and as those sounds faded away the wind in the trees and their footsteps against the rocks were all they could hear. It was beautiful here, the tall trees cozy around them...the view of the valley below stretching out forever. It was the perfect place for a picnic!

Jake and Molly enjoyed their sandwiches and chatted, watching the birds and squirrels busy all around them. As they ate the wind changed, and began to blow a little stronger and colder, and all of a sudden...it was snowing! "This is magical Jake!" his Mom whispered and Jake agreed. They leaned their backs up against the tree that was protecting them and snuggled together, warm and safe.

Jake thought this was probably the most delicious apple he'd ever tasted, and munched happily with juice running down his chin. His Mom laughed and wiped the juices off his face with a napkin. "A pretty great lunch eh Jake?" Molly asked.

Jake smiled his big, shining smile and hugged her tight. "As long as I live Mom, I will never forget this day! This is the very BEST surprise day EVER!"

Sniffer

Sniffer was worried. The Golden Retriever paced back and forth in the living room, stopping now and then to look out the window. "Where is my boy?" she wondered. Sniffer loved her Jake; and would do anything for him and she felt it was her job to protect him always. Today he had gone off without her because she had been at the Vet, and her Vet wouldn't let children come with their pets to visits. She had been home a long time now though, and Jake still wasn't here. Sniffer was worried.

She lifted her head and cocked it to the side, listening. Her silken tail began to move side to side...slowly... anticipation building because she heard "the car". Molly's car, and that might mean Jake was coming too! They weren't home when Uncle Mark dropped her off from the Vet, and she had been waiting ever since. Waiting... she was so good at waiting.

She made soft sounds in her throat now, and ears fully at attention. Now whining with excitement; her tail moving faster and faster!

The screen door creaked open. Sniffer yipped and ran for one of her toys to offer to the family to show her pleasure at their return. The door opened carefully; her people knew she would be close on the other side and they didn't want to hurt her with the door. She quivered with joy! There they were! Molly and Jake.

Her precious boy!!! She lay down on the floor with him and gave him a quick bath, and he responded with laughter and hugs.

Now Sniffer was at peace again. Her people and her world were back in place. She and Jake lay on the living room rug, Jake's head on her tummy; using it as a pillow like he always did when he watched TV. Sniffer breathed a deep sigh of contentment. She slept.

The City

Jake's blue eyes sparkled with delight. He and Uncle Mark finished loading the suitcases into the trunk of the car and Jake was bombarding his Uncle with questions about the trip. "is it VERY far? should I take a book? how many times have you been there? is it fun? does Mom really like it?" Mark laughed his big booming laugh and ruffled Jakes's blonde hair with both hands. "You are really something Nascar 2" he noted, "I can't answer any of your questions...you don't give me a chance!" He chuckled at his 6 year old nephew. "

"I'm just so excited Nascar 1, I've never been to the city before!" he half-ran, half-walked toward the house. "I know you are little man, but just be patient though because its still quite a long drive." Mark smiled. "OK Uncle Mark, I'll try." said Jake, and his eyes twinkled and his wide smile never left his tanned little face.

Molly; Jake's Mom, Mark and Jake drove for about three hours. They sang songs and told stories, played eye-spy and had snacks. All of it was fun, but Jake couldn't stop thinking about "The City!" He wondered if he might see a police car chase, or a lady dressed in fancy clothes and diamonds, or a store with all the toys in the Universe!! Oh boy!!

It was Dark when they crested the hill. Millions of city lights twinkled below and in front of them; as far as the eye could see, and Jake caught his breath. "Wow" he slowly exhaled. "It's really beautiful isn't it honey?" asked his Mom. "I will never forget the first time I saw it and how amazing I thought it was!"

They arrived at the hotel and his Mom let him use the room key and open the door. Uncle Mark had the room beside theirs, and a special door connected the two rooms on the inside! "I want to hurry up and go to sleep Mom" Jake said matter-of-factly. "Really Jake, why is that?" Molly asked him. "So we can get up and order room service!" Jake chirped. Molly laughed and helped Jake get ready for bed. "I love you more" she said as she tucked him in and gave him a hug. "No, I love YOU more" replied Jake. This was the little exchange they had every night, no matter what. A quick kiss on the forehead and Molly sang,"Well, I love you MOST!"

Morning was bright and sunny and after a room service breakfast of muffins, fruit and milk the trio headed out on their adventure. An ambulance and fire truck screamed by with lights flashing as soon as they stepped out of their hotel, and all the sounds and smells of the big and busy city startled the blonde haired boy. "Is it always this loud?" he asked. "Yep, it's wild Jake" His Uncle laughed and drew his nephew to his side. "just stay with us and you'll be fine. You get used to it after a little while." he assured Jake.

Their day passed by with cab rides, a hot dog lunch from a man with a cart on the sidewalk, a visit to the biggest toy store Jake had ever seen, a trip to the zoo, and a ride on a small ferry boat; where Jake even got to sit in the Captain"s chair and help him pilot the boat across the water! Jake was getting hungry again, so he was very happy when his Mom said it was time for dinner. They ate their dinner in a special restaurant that was at the very top of a building...and the restaurant rotated!!! In the time it took to eat dinner, they went around twice, and as they moved...dusk and then darkness came...and they saw the same beautiful display of twinkling lights as the night before. Jake started to get very sleepy, and so they took a cab back to their hotel and had another terrific night's sleep.

Jake and his Mom stayed in their room and Jake watched cartoons in bed; he was never allowed to do that at home! Uncle Mark went and completed his city business, and then it was time to go home. It was a beautiful sunny day, and once they were far from the city, Uncle Mark pulled off the road to a rest stop by a wild river. They ate a delicious lunch that Uncle Mark got as a surprise," from my favourite Deli in all the city!"

Jake was so happy to see their house and their lake. Sniffer had been with their neighbour, and she came running to meet the truck as they came down the driveway... a small trail of dust cloud behind them. Sniffer and her boy greeted each other with squeals of delight, hugs and big licks all over Jake's face! the little boy was so happy to be back with his puppy!

Jake sat down with Sniffer, his arm around her silky neck, and gazed out at "their" lake. He had really enjoyed their trip to the city; and all the things, people and adventures the trip included. He really loved that he went on a "road trip" with his Mom and Uncle...and he would never forget the music, singing, laughing and fun they had. But Jake knew something for sure. This was home...and home was the best place of all.

The Cousins

Jake woke up and smiled. He could see the sun shining through the window and that meant he and his cousins could be outside again today! They were visiting him for a whole week, and it was half OVER! He loved them, and they always had so much FUN when they were together; and this visit they were building a fort by the lake! Lucy and Ben were closer his age, and then Cora and Alice were younger, but they all worked together and were having the BEST time!!

After a breakfast of pancakes and orange juice, the band of cousins headed to the lake shore with Sniffer leading the way and Wesley and Clarence; his cousin's dogs, ambling along behing them. The big waves from last night's wind storm had done a little bit of damage to their creation, so they got right to work cleaning that up, and then they got back to building their Fort.

Everyone had important jobs. Cora and Alice gathered long grasses and soft willow branches to use for tying branches and poles together. Ben made sure the top pole was secure between the two trees. Jake leaned the poles for the walls into position and Lucy tied them all tightly. Then the crew gathered old leaves and made the floor of their fort soft and comfy, and they spread an old blanket on top to hold it all in place! It was really coming along, and they were all hot and dusty from their hard work.

"Time for a swim!" they chorused, and headed for the house to get permission, supervision, and change into their bathing suits. The adults were happy to take a break from all their chores and head to the lake for a swim as well. Everyone had a wonderful time swimming; with inner tubes, noodles, and taking turns in the paddle boat, and then back to the house for a quick lunch. The "Cousin Crew" cleaned up the kitchen and then back to their fort!

Jake's Mom gave them an old tarp she had in storage and it was so big it covered the entire fort perfectly! They tied it snugly and even put rocks all along the bottom so it would stay tight against the poles, and when they crawled inside it was warm, cozy, and protected from the wind off the lake.

The adults built a bonfire on the beach and helped them to have a weiner roast for dinner, and the band of cousins ate their dinner in the fort while the adults all sat around the bonfire talking, laughing, and listening to music. The cousins all decided this was the best thing they'd ever built! Uncle Mark said it was called a "lean-to", but they all called it THE FORT.

A Regal Visitor

Jake had been busy all morning, cleaning his room and doing his kitchen chores. He loved having his room tidy and getting the dishes dried and put away, but he could hear the birds singing outside and the gentle breeze that blew through the screen door smelled fresh and clean, and Jake could hardly wait to get outside and enjoy the day!

The slender 8 year old stopped by the door and hiked up his jeans with one hand. He hoped the new belt his Mom had ordered him would keep his pants from slipping down! The breeze gusted through the door, ruffling his blonde hair, and Jake peeked out the door at the gorgeous and sunny day that awaited him.

He drew in a delighted breath at the glorious sight that greeted him. He was back! Jake was so happy! The Visitor hadn't been there for a couple of weeks, and Jake and his Mom Molly were concerned that maybe he had moved on, but there he was... laying peacefully in the shade of the flowering bushes that Molly had planted all around their yard.

Jake opened the screen door carefully, and moved slowly to the chair right by the door on the porch. "Hello" he said gently. "I'm so glad you're back, and that you're enjoying the shade in our yard" The Regal Visitor lay calmy on the cool grass, his watchful eyes never leaving Jake's face, and his ears twitching in little wee movements at the sound of Jake's voice.

Jake knew not to leave the porch. The visitor seemed gentle and calm, but his Mom said he was a wild animal and Jake was NOT to leave the porch or go near him. That was ok with the small boy, he was happy to sit quietly and share a visit with such an amazing animal.

Molly came out onto the porch and sat in the other chair. "hello, big fella,' she whispered to their friend. "So nice to see you again" She smiled. "He looks happy there Jake...I wonder if he has found the apples yet?" Molly wondered.

As if he understood her, the huge buck deer stood up and raised his nose into the air...smelling...nose wrinkling...ears twitching. He walked gracefully around the side of their house to the waiting feast! Apples from their trees scattered all over the grass, just the kind of tasty treat a deer loved! Jake and his Mom sat on the porch and chatted to each other and to the big deer while he munched and crunched his way through a half dozen apples.

Then there was a noise and his head shot up. A car approaching down the driveway. With one leap, he was over the fence and moving toward the trees. He stopped, and turned his head back toward where Jake stood on the porch. Jake waved to him, and the regal visitor disappeared into the trees, tummy full of apples. The small boy felt very thankful their friend felt safe enough to come here, and he couldn't wait for his next visit!

Printed in the United States
by Baker & Taylor Publisher Services